Holly
Woodsnoff
and the Oddball Neighbor

Holly Woodsnoff

and the Oddball Neighbor

Adele Ciociola

Holly Woodsnoff and the Oddball Neighbor
Copyright © 2018 by Adele Ciociola

This is a work of fiction. The names, characters, places, or events used in this book are the product of the author's imagination or used fictitiously. Any resemblance to actual people, alive or deceased, events or locales is completely coincidental.

Book design by Maureen Cutajar
www.gopublished.com

ISBN-13: 978-0-9980348-0-5
ISBN-10: 0-9980348-0-0

Acknowledgements

IN 5ᵀᴴ GRADE, I wrote two short stories about neighbors —
The Nosy Neighbor and *The Oddball Neighbor*. And in a
very motherly fashion, my mom loved both and strongly
encouraged me to continue working on them. She reached
out to her author friend, Anna Bendewald, for a recom-
mendation on a writing coach, and Anna said that she
would love to mentor me herself!

In our first meeting at the Barnes & Noble at The
Grove, Anna said she would help me turn one of my
stories into a book if I was up for it and I was like, "This is
gonna be EPIC." She taught me how to write a balanced
story, about perspective, character development and
building suspense. She read my book countless times and I
can't thank her enough for being The Best Editor Ever!

I want to thank Mr. Ostrom, my 5th grade English
teacher, in whose class I originally wrote this story as an

11-page short story. I also want to thank all of my truly exceptional English teachers: Ms. Gooden ("Class, commas are your friends, unless you're Adele.") and Ms. Mathewson.

Thank you to my mom who has a "bottomless energy and enthusiasm for all my endeavors" (my dad's words). She read the entire *Harry Potter* series to me the summer before 1st grade. That series turned me into the reader I am today. I also want to thank J.K. Rowling and Hermione, Harry and Ron for teaching me the importance of friendship, courage and loyalty. Thanks to my friends, many of whom have been by my side since 1st grade and inspired the characters of Harper and Xailoh: Kalliopi, Lily, Roen, Hayden, Izzy, Ulara, Leah, Ava, Bella, and Sabrina.

I'm lucky to have such a creative and supportive family. My grandma not only read my draft but gave me a deeper understanding of my own story! She's also a talented artist and designed my cover. Tia Donna, Tia Ana and cousin Erika read my draft and gave me feedback. Grandpa got to page 13, and Tio Felipe says he'll "read" it when the audio book comes out. And while my dad still hasn't read my book, I want to acknowledge him for helping me in every other way imaginable. And of course, my mom, my biggest fan.

Lastly, my dear reader, I want to thank YOU for reading my book! I would be even more eternally grateful if you went to Amazon and left me a review. Getting reviews helps other people find books by new authors like me. If you're not used to writing reviews, it can be as simple as mentioning which character was your favorite. Thank you so much for your support!

Holly Woodsnoff

and the Oddball Neighbor

Chapter 1

BRIGHT FLASHING LIGHTS, loud crashing sounds and shocking vibrations. *That* is what I experience every night. *Annoying, right?* Do you know where this is all happening? In my bedroom! And do you know where it's coming from? My next door neighbor's townhouse. Not to mention my room has the *thinnest*. walls. **ever.** It's like the builder mixed glue and water to create these papier-mâché walls.

Now before I continue, let me give you some background. For starters, my name is Holly Woodsnoff. I live in a townhouse in Santa Monica, California. We live in the front unit facing the street and for as long as I can remember, no one has ever inhabited the unit behind us. All of that changed about a month ago when an 80 or 90-something-year-old man named Mr. Fletcher moved in next door. My life has not been the same since.

I'm currently twelve, turning thirteen in nine days! I have decorated my room to fit my personality; which is anything fluffy, colorful, aesthetic, sparkly and sweet scented. So there's glitter, *lots* and *lots* of glitter! My eyes get moony just thinking about how perrrr-fect my room is!

As much as I absolutely love my room, Mr. Fletcher's odd way of living really affects the good vibes my room *should* be giving off, and that is very distracting. It's just that his oddness is so powerful, it doesn't stay contained in his three-story house, and it wanders into my, if I do say so myself, fabulous room. Uninvited!

Good, now that we have that out of the way, I can get on with my story. A few weeks ago, my parents and I were eating pizza from Joe's Pizza because no one felt like cooking. It was quiet (as it always is) because fortunately for me I have no brothers or sisters to create outlandish, unnecessary noise. Fletcher, excuse me, *Mister* Fletcher unlocked the door as he does everyday at precisely five o'clock in the evening after rattling the old locks by playing tug-of-war with his keys and the door (which is probably just as old, if not older than he is). When he finally got inside his townhouse, he said in his husky British accent, "I'm home!" which received no answer. We heard him as he continued to recount his day until he finally shut his front door and blocked out the sound. This loud ritual has continued at five o'clock on the dot every day since.

While this ritual is a real nuisance, the really peculiar thing about him announcing "I'm home!" was that we knew he lived alone. In fact, I don't think we've ever seen him with another living object. Hmmm … ? My parents and I started brainstorming and they listened intently as I wondered aloud, "An old man who supposedly lives by himself, who I've never seen with anyone, or seen talk to anyone, not a friend or a neighbor, no pets, no roommates. What's up with the obnoxious strobe lights and loud noises coming from his home? How can one old man make such a ruckus? I've also noticed the gold bracelet he wears, it once reflected the sunlight and nearly blinded me! And why is his back always to me? Just once, I'd like to see his creepy face and beady eyes up close."

My mom let out a gasp, "Honey, how do you know he has a creepy face if you've never actually seen it?"

"You can totally tell. But nevermind that, I'm going to write a letter to the City of Santa Monica complaining about the noise and bright lights. There must be some ordinance against it," I announced in a confident tone.

"Oh sweetie, that is not necessary … un—" my mother paused.

"Holly, dear, it's best for you to just mind your own business and leave him alone," my dad gave me a serious look. I continued asking mental questions, which was why I was too busy to question the look my parents exchanged.

"May I be excused?" I said. I went up to my room to continue my thoughts in private. Who is this guy from England (I'm guessing based on the accent) and why is he living in Santa Monica? I took out my holographic pen, a stack of long marble sticky notes and wrote at the top, "Odd Things Mr. Fletcher Is Doing." Then I had an idea and called my best friend Harper.

"Hey you," Harper said on the other end of the phone.

"Hey," I repeated after a pause, "You know how you evicted your downstairs neighbor last year?"

"Uh-huh," she said, a bit distracted.

"Harper … if you're playing video games while talking to me I would like to let you know that I need your *full* attention."

"Sorry, what?"

Harper's my best friend in the world, but she can sometimes be sooooo clueless in a crisis situation.

"Oh right. Okay, so what were you saying?"

After I heard the sound that video games make when someone dies I continued, "Your neighbor who you evicted … " I waited.

"Yeah, Mr. Vic."

"What did you have to do exactly?"

"I don't know, it was all my parents," she responded bored.

"Thanks, soooo helpful," I retorted sarcastically.

"Really?" Harper sounded surprised.

Ugh, you really are so clueless sometimes! I thought to myself as I gently hit the palm of my hand against my head. "Anyway, do you at least know *what* you evicted him for?"

"Obvi, a few months after he moved in downstairs, we started receiving creepy notes on our doorstep, things like 'Karma's gonna get you.' My dad put up a camera to find out who it was and we caught him on video!"

"Oh-k … " I started to say, but Harper just kept barreling right on ahead.

"My dad took the video to the police and Mr. Vic said we were the worst neighbors he's ever had the displeasure of living below. He said it was like living near the Santa Monica Roller Coaster."

"How rude!" I heard boys screaming on the other end of the line and to protect my ears, I quickly wrapped up the conversation, "Anyway, thanks, and see ya tomorrow!"

"Okay, see you tomorrow," and the line went dead.

All I need to do is catch Mr. Fletcher in the act of doing something creepy. But first, dessert.

Chapter 2

I WANDERED DOWNSTAIRS into the kitchen to see if we had any of my mom's birthday cake left. As I opened the fridge, I saw the cat themed calendar hanging on the fridge above the water dispenser. This month's cat had on a red hat and a black mustache, and underneath said, "cats meowside how bout dat." On today's date, it read "Xailoh 7pm." As I pondered what that meant, the doorbell rang, followed by my mom yelling, "Honey, Xailoh's here to work on your science project."

Shoot, shoot, shoot. I was supposed to have all the supplies ready and some questions drafted. I needed to stall. I ran out to the doorway and pulled Xailoh into the kitchen. He was all business, taking out his laptop and placing it on the kitchen table.

"Want some cake?" I said trying to butter him up.

"Okay."

"Just help yourself while I go get everything," I said, pointing to the fridge. I thought, *Okay, so in my room I have markers, gems, glitter, hot glue gun, foam paper. Wait, I don't have foam paper! Maybe Mom has some in her closet ...*

I walked out of the kitchen, through the marble-floored foyer and up the stairs. I went into the crafts room, which doubled as my mom's office. I headed toward the closet on the far right of the room, my feet sinking into the soft, white alpaca rug we brought back from Peru last year. When I reached the crafts closet, I opened up the mirrored sliding door, and started pulling out black-lidded boxes. I reached for the top box that was closest to the wall, opened a lid and found my artwork from preschool. *Nice stick figures,* I chuckled. Luckily the other boxes had white labels (mom is so organized!) and I didn't have to go through each one, one at a time.

Once I got to the fourth stack of boxes in the back of the closet, I found the box labeled "paper." I pulled the box out by the fabric handle and took the lid off. Inside, I found, not just the foam paper I was looking for, but construction paper, glitter paper, and iridescent paper.

I left the room hauling the paper basket along with me. Who knew how heavy paper could be! I walked into the hallway then down the stairs. When I finally reached the kitchen table, arms completely numb, I set the basket down and took a seat, feeling I had overexerted myself. *Did I ever shut the closet door? Aw, shucks, I don't think I did.*

"Sorry, Xailoh, I forgot something!" I jumped out of my seat and dashed back up the stairs.

"It better be the poster board," he yelled back after me.

Oops, I thought. When I got to my mom's office, I shut the sliding door and was about to leave when I saw a little doll house in my peripheral vision. I pivoted my foot, and went over to get a closer look. The house was sitting under my mom's desk, partially hidden by the swivel chair. I pulled the chair out of its place in the desk and gave the doll house a closer look. I peered through the windows of the house and saw that the doll house had exquisite detail, and looked sort of like our townhome but a lot smaller. *Huh that's, interesting …*

When I returned empty-handed, Xailoh said, "Where's the poster board?"

"Yeah," I said slowly trying to think of an excuse but couldn't. "About that … I don't have any so I'll have to buy some tomorrow."

"Okay, then, let's go through the survey questions I wrote," Xailoh emphasized the word "I" as he turned his screen towards me.

I pretended to read them but didn't have the mindspace to think about social media habits and attitudes right now.

Xailoh could tell I wasn't into it and asked if I had anything to add. I shook my head and he gave me a look like I wasn't carrying my weight on this project.

"Sorry I'm so distracted, but the problem I'm having with my odd next door neighbor has been all-consuming."

His look went from unhappy to doubtful. I needed him to understand and told him all about Mr. Fletcher and my call with Harper. When I finally finished my story, I was out of breath, but realized I had unintentionally run out the clock.

"Shoot, I have to get home. Glad we were able to get so much done," he said sarcastically. "I'll send you the link to the final survey tonight, and this part is important: I need you to send it out to everyone you know, okay, Holly?"

"I'll do that and I'll get the poster board tomorrow, I promise." He grabbed his bag and ran out the door.

As soon as he left, my mind turned to Mr. Fletcher. I took out my holographic pen and started a list.

Odd Things Mr. Fletcher Is Doing:

1. Neon colored strobe lights
2. Creepy music
3. Loud vibrations
4. Talking to people who do not exist

Solution

I stared at "Solution" for several minutes and started dozing off until I was abruptly awoken by slamming sounds that literally shook my room. I tugged at my lamp string to turn my light off and was startled by the neon lights pulsating through my paper thin wall. I fell into bed on my stomach and buried my head underneath my pillow to try and block out the lights and the sounds. When my mom came in much later to give me a kiss goodnight, all was calm again and I was finally able to fall asleep.

Chapter 3

"*BEEP, BEEP, BEEP,*" ugh, I groaned, peering through my thick brown hair soaked in globs of drool. I went to hit my alarm clock but ended up knocking it off my weathered white bureau. I rolled out of bed, though it was more of a fall that ended with me banging my elbow on the ground.

"Ouch, that's going to bruise," I muttered under my breath as I crawled through the piles of clothes over to my alarm clock, which was resting upside down on top of the blue science fair form. I picked it up, banged the Off button and all was wonderfully silent again. But I knew I had to boogie.

"Holly, if you don't get up this instant you are going to be late for school!" I scolded myself, "Again!" I quickly pulled on my clothes, a white shirt with lace flowers around the neckline and ruffles midway down the arm, paired with black workout leggings I found at the top of my drawer. I hurriedly brushed my hair and pulled it up into pigtails, no time to pin them into space buns. I grabbed my backpack, phone, lunch box, water bottle, as well as my homework. Then I dashed downstairs and through the hallway, yelled, "Bye!" without waiting for a response and ran out the door.

Exiting towards the back of the building and down the stairs to the garage to get my bike, I had to walk right past Mr. Fletcher's front door. I paused for a moment and glanced at the chipping moss green paint. If we ever happen to be leaving at the same time, then we are *going* to have to interact. Lovely.

I hopped on my bike and after ten minutes of biking really fast, I was out of breath and decided to glide the rest of the way. When I finally arrived at school, it was completely silent.

"Was school canceled for a teacher's conference?" I wondered aloud as I pushed through the front doors. Then I saw Mr. Letterman, the English teacher and head of the school newspaper, attaching flyers to the bulletin board.

"You're here early, Holly!" he said.

I swiveled around to face him, "Really?" *It couldn't be any earlier than 8:00 and considering school started at 8:05 I wasn't really that early.*

"Well it *is* 7:02," he said.

"Wait! *What?*" I hurriedly pulled out my phone and sure enough it was 7:02. *What the h-e- double hockey sticks am I going to do with all this time?*

I don't understand why my alarm went off so early, but I bet Mr. Fletcher had something to do with it!

"What are you doing here so early, Mr. L?" I asked.

"I'm finishing up this month's issue of the school newspaper, but I still need one more story," he said his eyebrows dancing, "Have you given any more thought to my offer?"

My reflex reaction was the same as every other time he had asked me, "Mr. L, you know I am way too busy with dance, my DIY business … stalking my neighbor." But I didn't say that last part.

He sighed, "Oh-kay but if you change your mind, you'll always have a spot on the newspaper team."

"Thanks. I'll think about it," I said through a forced smile, knowing that I had no intention of giving it another thought. I started heading through the eerily silent hallways towards my locker. The only people I saw were teachers scurrying off towards the printer room, or running out of the building looking around to make sure no kids or parents were following them. "Probably heading off to get Starbucks," I muttered with a chuckle, not remembering the last time a teacher taught a class without caffeine of some sort.

When I finally reached my locker I turned the dial and the door popped open. Chills went down my spine every time I saw my locker, it was just soooo pretty!! I had covered the three inside walls with marble vinyl paper and lights that turned on when I opened the door. There was also a disco ball, pink shag rug, mirror, and sparkly magnets. If the school held a locker contest (which they totally should) I would definitely win. I wrote 'Buy Poster Board" on the whiteboard, then as I reached for my notebook, a piece of paper fluttered onto the ground. I lowered myself onto the ground and saw that it was just a piece of blue-lined notebook paper with scribbly hand-writing on it.

Meet me by the lemon tree before school, need to talk about OUR science project!

Oh Xailoh, how is it that no matter how early I get to school, you still manage to get here before me? I stuffed the paper into my bag, slammed my locker shut (something I can only do on the rare occasion that I'm early and no one's around) then walked to the lemon tree outside of the school where most people carpool.

"You're here early," Xailoh said when I rounded the corner, he was lying on the grass with his head resting on his backpack as a pillow. There was an impish grin on his face.

"Just be happy I could be here at all, considering I'm *always* late," I said with a smile.

The grin on Xailoh's face just kept growing larger and all of a sudden, my sleepy fog lifted, "Wa, wa, wait … YOU tampered with my alarm clock!"

"I can't believe it actually worked. But I'm glad it did because we really need to talk about *our* science project, you know, the one where I've done all the work so far," he gave me a chastising look while running his fingers through his dyed blue hair that's ridiculously long in the front.

"Okay, but first … "

"Coffee. Yes, I know," then he laughed.

"But first," I said trying not to smile, "You really need to cut your hair, like now."

"Uh, no way, how about I cut *your* hair."

"How dare you! My first dance competition is less than a month away," I said patting my long brown hair adoringly. Only 26 days to be exact before I'm up on stage competing. My body seized up every time I thought about it.

"Anyway, getting back to science, did you send the survey out to all of your friends like you said you would?"

"Uh," I paused trying not to let the uncertainty creep into my voice, "of course I did."

Unfortunately, Xailoh saw right through it. "Holly," he said giving me one of his stares that may as well be a truth potion.

"Okay, honestly, I forgot but I'll do it right now," I took out my phone and posted it to my Instagram story, added the link to my bio and sent a text to all my friends.

"Okay, done!"

"And what about the poster board?"

"I'm getting that tonight."

"Holly, that's what you said on Friday!" he said arching his eyebrows (which were brown, not blue).

"Did I say that? I really don't recall, I think you're making things up now," I said tilting my head to the right, giving the impression that I felt sorry for him.

"Did Holly Merengue Woodsnoff, really just say that to me?" he said grinning from ear to ear, his eyes sparkling with mischief and his dimples going very deep. He grabbed me by the arm and was holding his water bottle over my head, I felt my mouth form an "O" shape then, I felt something cold trickle onto my hair then drip into my eyes. An ice cube hit me on the forehead.

"Oh no you didn't," and in a flash I grabbed the water bottle out of his hands and sprayed him back. I ran away screaming, "I'll buy the poster board tonight and you can quote me on that!"

I dashed off to class realizing there were only ten minutes until school started. Kids were starting to flood the halls, which would make it *impossible* to get to my locker if I waited any longer. I rushed past kids pushing and shoving, knowing that Xailoh was probably hot on my tail. When I reached my locker, I quickly spun the dial but it didn't open. I tried the combination again but it was too late—I felt several ice cubes rolling down my back.

"Xailoh how dare you!" I shouted as I turned around to see him running off. I finally got my locker open, grabbed my stuff and headed off to homebase, plotting how I would get back at him.

Chapter 4

WHEN I WALKED into homebase (two minutes early), Xailoh was already in his seat, directly in front of me with his feet propped up on the desk in front of him, looking smug. *Where was Harper anyway?* I ripped a piece of paper out of my holographic notebook (available for purchase at HollyDIYs.com) and scribbled a note:

I'll get you back when you least suspect it.
Bwahahahahahahahahah

I then walked to the front of the classroom toward my teacher's desk, "conveniently" bumping into Xailoh's desk and "accidently" dropping the piece of paper onto the light brown faux wood surface.

"Oops, sorry," I said covering my mouth with my hand and pretended to be sorry.

Xailoh looked up, giving me a look that said he wasn't buying it.

"Must've dropped that," I pointed to the paper. "Oh well, you can keep it," I said shrugging, then proceeded to loop around the center section of the three rows of tables back to my seat.

As I settled into my seat I saw Harper enter the room and take her seat on my right. She looked at me then Xailoh, lastly her eyes wandered back to me "What'd he do now?"

"Poured water on me AND ice cubes!" I said not meeting her gaze.

"By the looks of it, you may have done some water pouring yourself."

"Me?" I said pointing to my heart, "I would never!" I exclaimed.

Harper rolled her eyes and said, "Yeah, and I would *never* steal gummies from your lunch either."

She smiled and crossed her eyes. We broke out into a fit of giggles. Just then the bell rang and in walked our teacher. The class became dead quiet, and everyone rolled their shoulders back and sat up, with good posture. Xailoh also took his feet off the chair in front of him, in which sat the teacher's pet and know-it-all, Charles. His face crumpled up in disgust at Xailoh's dirty shoes and deciding he needed hand sanitizer, he raised his hand.

"Yes, Charles?" the teacher asked.

"Can I please get up to get hand sanitizer? After all, the classroom is a breeding ground for germs that cause colds and flus," he enlightened us all. Eye roll.

"Oh yes, of course, Charles. You are correct. This being flu season and all, it is extremely important to wash and sanitize your hands frequently," she glanced adoringly at Charles who had stalked over to the smart board in the front of the class, his heels clicking on the wooden floor. He turned right at the smart board, over to the mini bookshelf that held the mega large hand sanitizer. He looked directly at Xailoh and pumped five squirts into his hands, then massaged it in carefully. I rolled my eyes again.

Xailoh turned around and said, "That's it?" with mock outrage, "Last time it was six!" He then gave me a goofy smile, which I returned, but my eyes were still threatening, reminding him that this war wasn't over yet. *Oh how dramatic I can be. Isn't it wonderful?* I thought with a chuckle.

BEEEEEEEEP, the bell rang out through the classroom, letting us know that it was time for our next period. Everybody pushed and shoved their way out of the room, except Charles, of course. He just had to follow the teacher in everything down to how to hold your freaking pencil.

He sat in his seat patiently listening to all the exciting announcements Ms. Paley delivered.

My stomach was growling from waking up so early and skipping breakfast, but I would have two more classes to endure before lunch. I dreaded math because we were having a quiz and my desk partner, Tristan, is so distracting. He can't help but whisper every word problem out loud, instead of using his reading skills that he learned in, I don't know, *Kindergarten!* I normally tune him out, but today I was in no mood. I asked him to use his silent reading skills, and he shot back at me. This quickly escalated into a whisper argument with a lot of scary facial and hand expressions to earn us some interesting stares from the rest of the class. Meanwhile the teacher didn't even notice what was happening. However, the minute I tried to end the argument by getting up to get a new pencil from her supply closet, the teacher immediately looked up.

"Holly, can I help you with something?"

"My pencil broke and I need to get a new one."

Without saying a word, she held out her hand and put on her reading glasses. I stood frozen as she examined my pencil from every possible angle as the minutes ticked away. She conducted her very tedious examination of my pencil to make absolutely sure it was sufficiently broken to warrant a new one. Nevermind that she has boxes and boxes of brand new pencils in her supply closet. And nevermind that I needed to get back to my quiz!

I could tell she wasn't convinced so I spoke up, "Ms. Kapley, my pencil is so dull, it's like writing with a stone. I know you don't like us using the pencil sharpener during class. So if you would allow me to get a new pencil, I will be able to finish—"

"Oh, Holly, after careful inspection, it is clear to me that this pencil is still highly functioning and not at all broken. Now please go back to your seat and finish your quiz."

I avoided eye contact but could feel Tristan's gloating stare as I went back to my desk.

From math, I went to social studies where we were learning geography. We played a game where the teacher randomly selected a location in the world and we took turns answering whether it was a continent, country, state or city. If you got it wrong, you had to take your seat. The first time we played this game, every single student even Xailoh got out in the first round.

"Clearly we'll be leading the United Nations one day," Xailoh said sarcastically. I giggled.

Finally the bell rang again and it was lunch time. However, instead of heading toward the lunchroom, I went to the girls bathroom to plot my revenge on Xailoh.

I found a small container of clear slime and a bag of plastic spiders and worms at the bottom of my backpack left over from Halloween. I moved them to the outside pocket for easy access. *I knew these would come in handy one day,* I thought to myself.

As I walked past the cafeteria, I saw today's smoothie was blueberry. I was still looking at the sign when I collided with Xailoh, "Hi Xailoh!" I said cheerfully when I reached our regular table outside the cafeteria. It was the best spot because the grass was right next to it and it was hidden by the handball court, so Harper and I could practice acrobatics without getting caught. "I noticed they have your favorite blueberry smoothie today—let me take your lunch while you get one?"

"Uh, sure," he said skeptical of my motives, as he turned to leave.

"Okay," I said indifferently, trying not to give away how pleased I was. Harper was already sitting at the table munching on her sandwich.

"Holly, why are you holding Xailoh's lunch?" she asked knowing I was up to no good. I ignored her question, and took out my supplies. I put the spider and worms in the slime and applied a thin layer of water to make it extra gross.

"Pay back time!" I replied after a minute, as I dropped the slimy critters into his lunch bag with the peanut butter and jelly sandwich he has eaten everyday, without fail, since the 4th grade.

When he came back he was empty handed, with a sly smile on his face, "Uh Holly."

"Yes," I said casually.

"There wasn't a blueberry smoothie today," he said not at all surprised.

I thought back to the computerized sign, it had said blueberry … right?

"It was a *black*berry smoothie," he said sounding annoyed. "You know what, just forget it. Let's just eat our lunch."

Harper, using one of her many skills, was acting oblivious to what was going on said, "What did you get on your math test?"

Harper almost never asks about grades since Xailoh and I are the competitive ones. Her bringing up the test must mean she did really well.

Before I could respond, she said beaming with joy, "I got 25/25!"

"That is so great, Harper! Let's go to Pinkberry this week to celebrate!" I said happily. I looked over at Xailoh for his reaction. *Why did he seem mad at me, I hadn't done anything that he knew of … yet.*

Chapter 5

I FELT A smile playing on my lips. Just then Xailoh let out a little yelp, and when I looked over he was frantically shaking his hands, like he was puppy fighting, "What the heck! What is that?" he said startled. Then calmly, he opened his lunch again for a better look. "Wait a minute," he paused and pulled it out, "it's fake!" he said exasperated. I was trying to keep my face poised and not laugh but I couldn't help it and I let out a laugh.

He stared right at me, "Ok, Holly, it is on. You better watch your back."

"Oh, no, that just makes us even."

He was about to argue, but at that moment, Annabella wandered over to our table, her Rapunzel blond hair and long, flowy purple dress billowing out behind her. Yes, she really does wear long dresses in different shades of purple almost everyday. It's like she's royalty, sure acts like she is!

"Hiya, Harper! Your 'Hi-Bye' hoodie is totes adorbs, LOL, pink is definitely your color, really works with your sun-kissed curls," said Annabella.

I forgot Harper and Annabella were once friends back in Kindergarten when they both danced on a team together. Annabella now rides horses. I started dancing in 3rd grade and that's when Harper and I became instant best friends.

"And, Holly, that bracelet with your name on it is just so, um, adorbs!" Before I can even say thank you, she waves her hands in front of us and blurts out, "Do you like my nails? They were, like, $20,000." Oh, I forgot to mention Annabella is house-covered-in-diamonds-rich. According to Harper, her grandparents were in the trucking business and made a modest living. It wasn't until their business went under, forcing them to sell everything, that they realized they were sitting on a fortune in land. The grandparents insisted that their kids and grandkids go to public school to keep them "grounded." If you can be grounded on the moon, then I guess their plan is working.

Annabella held up her nicely manicured hands, that seemed to have dots on them, but as she moved closer to us, I noticed large diamonds on the tips of her ring fingers and small diamonds on the moons of every other finger. I really wanted to act disinterested so she would leave but I couldn't understand how the large diamonds stayed on her ring fingers. I took her hand and turned it over to reveal an earring post and back that held it in place. *Un-freakin-believable.*

She picked up on my interest and kept on talking, "My mom and I got them done at The Salon in Beverly Hills. They closed just for us and served us fancy drinks and macaroons. I also got real gold leaf flakes on my toes," she said as she slipped her little princess feet out of her ballet flats to show us her pink toenails covered in "real gold".

"Wow," Harper said trying to be nice but truly bored by all of this. I don't know how they were ever friends. Annabella didn't seem to get the hint and just kept on talking. Talking about how her "neighbor" Mr. Jewels gave her $6,000 for her birthday, and how she put it towards her nails. Her neighbor just bought a new Bentley but can't even drive because he's like 400 years old so he needs a chauffeur to drive him around. Then we learn her so-called neighbor is also her grandfather. The way she talks about him you'd think he was the King of England or something. Wait, bad comparison, knowing her, he probably is.

Harper and I tried to coax her into leaving, however for some reason, Xailoh appeared genuinely interested in what she was saying. When he changed the subject over to science, I realized he had an ulterior motive. Last year,

Xailoh and I lost The Science Cup to Annabella and Charles. Xailoh was crushed and still hasn't gotten over it.

Annabella wouldn't disclose what they're doing this year but let him know they'd really outdone themselves. If the judges liked what they did last year, they were going to be totes amazed this year.

Xailoh looked so sad, "Holly and I haven't even started."

"Don't worry, you're brilliant and you'll do great," her eyes smitten. Then she pulled out a gold sleeve of macaroons from her Louis Vuitton tote bag (which is her version of a backpack) and gave them to Xailoh, "I got these at The Salon yesterday and I want *you* to have them." Emphasis on the word "you."

Xailoh looked like a giddy three-year old and after a little more chit-chat, Annabella *finally* left. Once she was out of earshot, I exploded, "Oh, my gosh, she is totally crushing on you. It's almost embarrassing to watch!" I then gave Xailoh exactly a second to offer me and Harper a cookie and when he didn't, I gave him a nudge, "Xailoh those cookies look REALLY good!"

"Oh, just take one already," he said coming out of his thoughts.

Harper and I proceeded to take a cookie each.

After the most annoying lunch ever, the rest of the day dragged on. I was already dreading having to meet up with

Xailoh tonight to work on science considering how seriously he's taking it.

When the final bell rang, everybody, teachers and all, dashed for the exit, trying to beat the rush of students and failing. On Mondays, Harper and I ride our bikes to our dance studio right after school. When we reached the bike racks, I shot Xailoh a text,

Meet me at my house at 6

I hopped on my rustic blue bike, and Harper on her shiny red bike, we peddled slightly uphill—my throat burning with the effort—to San Vicente where our dance studio was located. The studio is housed in a 5,000 square foot pool house behind the owner's mansion. The owner was a principal dancer with the American Ballet Theatre. Her name is Kameron, she has long brown perfectly wavy hair, big brown eyes and long limbs, kind of like a Disney princess. She teaches all the ballet classes. But today, I only have acrobatics with Miss Ashleigh.

Harper and I arrived 15 minutes early and started stretching. Sitting in butterfly, my thoughts drifted to my feud with Xailoh, my annoying neighbor Mr. Fletcher, and what is up with that doll house under my mom's desk? Harper tapped me on the shoulder and I looked up, "Come on, class is about to start," she said.

Class was awesome, 60 minutes of doing all sorts of crazy contortion moves with my partner who is always Harper. She's the best dancer on our team—she can do a million turns, the most perfect overextended center leaps and can walk a baseball diamond on her hands (she actually did that at her brother's game). But she's been at it since the age of four, I didn't start until the ripe old age of eight.

Class ended at five o'clock, which gave me an hour to get to the store, buy the poster board and get back to my house to meet Xailoh at six o'clock. I begged Harper to come with, but she had to go home.

At the store I was confronted with three different types of poster board—plain white, light blue and marble—I chose the marble one to add my own flair to the project.

The ride home would be mostly downhill. During the last stretch along Palisades Park, I could see the sun setting behind the mountains, and I could feel the cool ocean breeze on my face. I was relaxed by the time I reached my block. Not a care in the world.

But that quickly faded once I got to my doorstep. There were candles surrounding my entry way, like hundreds of them burning and putting out the most pungent odor. Had they been nice sage candles, that would have matched my mood. But this was a foul scent I couldn't even place. *This is Mr. Fletcher's handiwork. I'm sure of it. That's it, I have to come up with a plan for dealing with him. Tonight.*

I frantically blew out the candles. I checked my watch, Xailoh would be coming over in 15 minutes, but I really needed Harper at a time like this. I reached for my phone and begged her to come over, I sat on the stoop to wait for her. Not surprisingly, I could hear the sound of Xailoh's skateboard (*if you're on time, you're late is his motto*). At least the smell broke the ice between us.

"What in the heck is that awful smell?"

"I'll explain when we go inside. My parents aren't even home yet, so I asked Harper to come over, hope that's ok." He shrugged.

Harper arrived out of breath, the smile on her face quickly turned into an upside down smile, "You smell like something foul, girl," Harper exclaimed pinching her nose in between her fingers.

I ushered them both inside.

"Okay so you know, my neighbor, Mr. Fletcher?"

They both looked at me with blank stares.

"You know, the neighbor who just moved in behind us, the creepy old old man with beady eyes who is getting more and more bizarre by the day."

Now they both nodded.

"So basically, he's been doing a lot of *weird* things lately.

I tried to talk to my parents about him, but they just told me to stay away from him."

"I'm guessing this ... *strong* smell is courtesy of him?" Harper said raising her eyebrows.

"Yes. When I arrived home, there were hundreds of candles, just like, covering the entrance, and they were all lit, so I'm like uh, fire hazard, and immediately blew them out and disposed of them out back. Now my cute white top will need to be fumigated. I need to come up with a plan to deal with my crazy neighbor. Can you guys help me?"

"Yeah, let's start by figuring out what this scent is," Xailoh looked determined.

Chapter 6

TAP, TAP TAP, the three of us were sitting on the floor of my room, Googling disgusting candle smells, trying to figure out that unidentifiable scent. I wanted to ask my mom, who is a botanist but she was still not home, neither was my dad. I was getting concerned and texted them. No response.

After thirty minutes of searching online, Harper said, "I have narrowed it down to wolfsbane …"

"WOLFSBANE!" Xailoh blurted out. His voice got very quiet, "I read a comic book and it said wolfsbane is burned by witches, and anyone who isn't a witch can't even *touch* it without turning to stone immediately!" He sniffed the air. "Last year during science I took a test on the scents of things, and this was on the test. And if I'm correct, which I am, that is definitely the smell," he said with finality. "Which means that Mr. Fletcher must be a witch."

Harper gasped, "Well, that certainly explains all the odd things Mr. Fletcher has been doing."

"But why would Mr. Fletcher be burning it, what's the purpose?" I asked.

"In the comic book, it was used to ward off bad spirits or bad vibes, which can also be given off by people. You would put it in front of the door of a place that the bad spirits haunted, and they would leave."

"So you're saying there are bad spirits, or 'vibes' in our entryway? And are we talking ghostly vibes or human vibes?"

"Could be either. Do you get chills when you walk through, or will the camera not focus?"

"Uh, let's see," I grabbed my Instax Polaroid camera and ran downstairs to take a photo of my entranceway. Then I took another one of our foyer and another of the wall which Xailoh was leaning against. I set the film on the kitchen table and we watched it develop.

All the photos were in focus except the one with Xailoh in it. I started giggling as I saw a smudge on Xailoh's face, "I guess we found our bad spirit!"

"Oh really, are you sure a ghost named Hollywood didn't put that smudge on the lens?" he muttered under his breath and stormed out of the building and away to who knows where.

Harper and I looked at each other. "That escalated quickly!" I said exasperated.

"Yup, that's fo shizzles," Harper replied exhaling slowly, "are you going to apologize?"

"For what? I didn't do anything!" I crossed my arms.

"Don't act so innocent, Holly. Let's think … why might he be mad at you?"

"Ohhhh-kaaay, fine! Maybe because I told him there was a blueberry smoothie when there wasn't? But that was an honest mistake."

"I agree, that's not it … "

"Uhhhh, that I put that thing in his lunchbox?"

"Maybe, but you were just getting him back," Harper said.

"Ugh! Just tell me already!"

"Well, didn't you keep saying that you would work on the science project and you never did?"

"Maybe, but I've been dealing with one fire after another—literally," I said shrugging my shoulders.

"Oh no, that's *definitely it!*"

"Maybe," I said again even though I knew she was right. Obviously it was the science project. After we lost The Science Cup last year, he was so crushed, all I could say was "Just wait 'til next year" to cheer him up. Now we'll be lucky to get a passing grade.

"You know I'm right!" Harper exclaimed victoriously.

"I know … he stormed off before I could even show him the amazing poster board I got," I said bowing my head.

"Now will you *please please please* apologize to Xailoh?"

"Okay, you're totally right and I totally will, just not now. Right now I need to find my parents."

"What are you talking about?"

"I don't know if you've noticed, but we are completely alone in this house. I have no idea where my parents are. I've been texting them, but no response."

"Should we call the police?"

"They might get locked up for leaving me alone … Um, I know, I'll use Find My Phone to locate them."

"You know your mom's Apple ID!?" Harper couldn't believe it.

"She uses the same password for like, everything, so yeah."

I logged in as her and saw her iPhone on the map. That's when I really started freaking out, heart rate increasing. "She's at UCLA Medical Center!"

"What?! Try calling her again."

It rang and rang. I tried again and again. Finally my dad answered her phone

"Is Mom alright? What happened? Why haven't either of you called me?" I said.

"There's nothing to worry about Holly. We sent you a text earlier."

"I don't have any texts from you—NOT ONE!"

"There was a little hiccup, but we're on our way home now. See you in 20 minutes," he said.

"A little hiccup? What? No one goes to the hospital for hiccups!" *What was my dad not telling me?*

"Oh, it's just a manner of speaking, honey. Everything is fine. But … how did you know we were at the hospital?"

"Just come home, I need you here. Weird stuff has been happening and I'm starving. Oh, and Harper is here."

"Oh, I'm glad Harper's there with you. Love you, see you soon, honey," he said hanging up.

"You know, I'm not sure my dad would have told me he was at the hospital had I not brought it up. What is up with that?"

"Did he tell you what happened?"

"No, just that everything's fine and they'll be home soon. Now with that under control, let's get back to..."

Harper cut me off, "Apologizing to Xailoh."

"Actually I was going to say, my plan to deal with Mr. Fletcher." I took out my sticky note and added to the list.

Odd Things Mr. Fletcher Is Doing:
1. Neon colored strobe lights

2. Creepy music

3. Loud vibrations

4. Talking to people who do not exist

5. Tried burning our house down

I crumpled up the sticky note that said "Solution" and wrote this at the top of a new one. I know Xailoh called me Hollywood to make fun of me, but I actually like how it sounds. If I did have a detective agency, that's what I would call it.

Detective Hollywood's Plan

a. Set up a camera connected to my laptop to spy on him

b. Look through his garbage

c. Interview him

I showed Harper the list and said, "B is gross and C is terrifying so I guess it's going to be A."

"Really?"

"Harper, I'm kidding! We need to work on your gullibility. A and B are like, majorly invading his privacy and would probably land me in jail." We giggled. "I have no choice but to interview him, which means I would actually have to, deep breath, *talk* to him." I shuddered at the thought of him answering the door … his unkempt gray beard falling from his face, his mean eyes glaring down on me. (Insert face screaming in fear emoji.) At least that's what I assume he would look like, it's not like I have ever actually seen his face.

"So what's my cover going to be?" I thought outloud. "I could pretend to be doing a research project or to be a reporter or something … "

"What if you didn't have to pretend?"

"Go on."

Mr. Letterman's been offering you a job at the newspaper, right?"

"I guess. Wait, Harper You're a genius! Thanks!" I hugged her.

"No problem."

Just then headlights illuminated the kitchen window and I really hoped that meant my parents were home, with food. A few minutes later, they walked in with a huge bag from my favorite Indian restaurant. I started salivating.

"Hi honey, we're so sorry! We're just grateful Harper was here with you. We'll talk about it more tomorrow, okay? But right now, let's eat!"

We devoured the chicken curry and naan, then my dad took Harper home. I went upstairs to get ready for bed. I should have showered and washed my face but could barely muster the energy to brush my teeth. Then I hopped into bed, got under my cool sheets, and tugged at my night lamp. I lay in bed expecting the lights and sounds from next door to start blaring, but everything remained delightfully silent. My mom came in a few minutes later to give me a kiss goodnight. I hugged her tight. As she left the room, I thought it was strange that neither one mentioned the foul smell when they first entered the house. It was as if they already knew ...

Chapter 7

BEEP, BEEP, BEEP, ugh, you have got to be freakin' kidding me! I forgot to change my alarm back to seven. Well, I was awake. I headed to school early, again, and marched straight to Mr. L's office to take the job. Or more like the waiting room outside his office.

"I don't know how we are going to complete the school newspaper this month! I can't find anyone to do it." I overheard Mr. L telling the principal.

My eyes wandered over the bland yellowy beige walls, and the gray cushioned chairs. There were a total of six chairs, three on either side of the mini hallway. The floor was covered in blue tiles, dusty from all of the shoes walking through to Mr. L's office. My eyes landed on a fiddle-leaf fig plant that must have been fake, considering the only light was fluorescent ceiling lights.

I was getting a little impatient so I walked in front of

the door's window pane so he could see me. It worked, his eyes met mine and he opened it for me.

"Why, hello, Holly!" he led me into his very cheerful well lit office covered in pictures of him with his wife and twin girls. "I don't suppose you would like that newspaper job now, would you?"

"Actually that's the reason I'm here so early. Inspiration struck, and I think this is just what I need to do."

"Wonderful! We seem to have solved the problem, Mr. Letterman," the principal said, delighted to check this off her list. "If you will excuse me I'll let you get to work!"

Once she left, Mr. L said, "May I ask what suddenly inspired you to join the newspaper?" his eyes were curious.

I didn't have time for the truth, so I gave him the answer he wanted to hear, "You know how passionate I am about writing and would feel honored to write for the school paper."

"You don't know how pleased I am to hear you say that. For Friday, I'll need a personal interest story with a message. As you know there is a word count—400 words, okay?"

"Friday?" Oh gosh, that's the same day our science fair project is due, but what choice did I have? "Okay, Friday is great, as long as I can pick any topic I want."

He nodded and I took that as my cue to boogie. I headed

outside to the lemon tree, knowing Xailoh would be lying on the grass beneath it using his backpack as a pillow.

Honestly if you didn't feel the need to come to school sooooo early, you could lie in bed and have an actual pillow! I reasoned.

"Xailoh," I said in a singsong voice.

"Let me guess, you forgot to change your alarm clock?"

"No, of course not, I just voluntarily decided to wake up this early" I said sarcastically.

He laughed.

"Anyway I came to apologize for being so irresponsible about the science fair project, and anything else I may have done. However, I did notice I got quite a few survey responses... 492 to be exact, which means quite a bit of data for that thing you're always saying we need: statistical significance," I said with a proud smile.

"Sometimes you do listen. I also have to apologize for the alarm prank, the prank that just keeps on giving," he said smiling. "And before I accept your apology and lose the right to use the 'you need to apologize card' he smiled, "let's see all this data you're talking about."

"If you insist," I said pulling out my phone, and opening the Survey Monkey app.

"Woah! You got 497 people to answer it! How?" he asked clearly surprised.

"A few more than when I checked last night! I take it that means you forgive me, even though it was pretty obvious you had already forgiven me. And I just apologized for no reason," then we both laughed out loud. "Also, I got the most beautiful three-panel marble poster board. You are going to love it. Anyway I'll catch you later!" Then I ran off leaving him under the lemon tree. And headed to my locker to start working on the interview outline.

I took out my notepad, flipped to a new page, grabbed my holographic pen and started writing.

Mr. Fletcher Interview Outline

- What is your full name? (With this I might be able to find out more about him online)
- Where did you move here from? (Let's see if I was right about England)
- Why did you decide to move to Santa Monica?
- How old are you? (Impolite but there is NO way I am going to interview him and not get this question answered)
- Are you married? Do you have any children/grandchildren?
- What do you do for work?

- *Do you collect anything? (An indirect way of asking about the candles)*
- *Are you a wizard? (I wish I could ask this!)*

"Hi Holly!" Harper said as she approached. "You should probably get to class! Ms. Paley is about to suspend you for being late so often." *BEEEEEEEP!* The ten minute bell rang.

"Okay, but first let me tell you what I'm going to do," I quickly filled her in on my plan involving Mr. Fletcher.

"WHAT!!" Harper said at about 300 decibels, "Do you want me to come with you? I could bring my brother's little league bat, it's made of steel or something."

"Oh yes, why don't you just come with me, and bring Xailoh, too with his mom's boxing gloves. Ya know when Mr. Fletcher sees us, he'll instantly think, 'Yes! Come on in! Let's chat it out!'"

BEEEEEEEP! "That's the five-minute bell, better get going!"

As I dashed away Harper called out, "Thanks for letting us come!"

I turned around bumping into at least five kids hustling to their classes, then I continued running to homebase, knowing this day was going to drag on for eternities.

Chapter 8

BEEEEEEEEP! I slipped into my homebase seat just as the bell rang, eyes staring at Xailoh's back.

"Class," Ms. Paley began. "Before I get into today's announcements, we are going to be rearranging your seats." The class let out a moan. I personally was very pleased with my current seat, so I wasn't *thrilled* with this news.

The teacher put the seating chart under the smart board. I was being moved to the very last row, but thankfully, Harper's new seat was right next to mine.

The class didn't wait for permission and started shuffling around as Ms. Paley raised her voice, "Class, when you have figured out where your new seat is, you may gather your belongings and make your way there."

Harper and I exchanged a fist bump once we got to our seats. "I hope you will be able to make these seats work. If

you have any concerns, feel free to speak to me after class."
My classmates grumbled, but then settled down.

My teacher put the announcements on the smart board. When I looked up to read the board, the weirdest thing happened, it just looked like faint indistinct outlines of words. *Oh the smart board must be broken.* I walked up to the board to look at the text close up. Getting quite a few looks in the process, but of course I didn't care.

The paper read:

- **Report cards going home Friday**
- **Pick up class pictures from the office by Thursday**
- **Science fair projects due Friday**

I headed back to my seat, gathered my things and headed off to my next class.

As the day went on I encountered more broken smart boards, and that evening I mentioned it to my mom over chicken noodle soup. "Speaking of school, in homebase, history, and language arts, the smart boards were all broken."

"Really?"

"Everything was blurry," I explained.

She thought for a moment then asked, "Where do you sit in these classes?"

"Well, for homebase I just got moved to the very last row. For history I sit in the fourth row, and in language arts I had to sit with my partner, so again in the very last row."

"Hmm, but no blurriness in your other classes?" my mom clarified.

"Correct."

"Okay, and where do you sit in your other classes?"

"First and second row," I answered.

"Honey, I don't think the smart boards are broken." She took a deep breath, "It seems to me you need these handy appliances," she pointed to her glasses that were surrounding her eyes.

"So I need," it hit me, "I need *glasses?*" *Ah, so that's why I misread the smoothie sign.*

"Seems that way to me. I'll get you an appointment with my optometrist as soon as possible."

"ARGGG! Just not before Friday please." *I could not afford to add one more thing to my plate right now. Just think how wonderful my life will be after Friday, if I survive, that is.*

"Don't worry, we'll get you a nice stylish pink and sparkly pair that you love."

That wasn't what I meant, but no time to explain. When I was done with dinner, I asked to be excused then I went upstairs to work on the science poster. Xailoh had emailed me two data charts, which I reformatted to look prettier, then printed them out. Wow, the results were not at all what I had expected. I added our hypothesis, procedures and conclusion, and laid out the information in the most aesthetically pleasing way possible. I stood up and marveled at the feng shui of it. But before I could glue it down, the thumping sounds and blaring lights from next door started up again.

He better be done by the time I'm ready for bed! I went to the bathroom, and closed the door for peace and quiet. I took a nice long shower, meticulously brushed my teeth and even flossed. Thankfully, it was quiet when I opened the door to my room. My parents came up and tucked me in. I knew I was forgetting to do something but felt too tired to care.

Chapter 9

THE THING I forgot to do was change my alarm back to 7am. Wednesday started a lot like Tuesday and I was starting to realize 6am would be my new wake up time. *So today is Wednesday and my newspaper story is due Friday, which means I should probably do the interview... today! Oh great.* The more I thought about it, the more nervous I got. I reluctantly got out of bed and took my time getting ready.

As I had expected, the day dragged on and on. Meaning that when the final bell rang releasing me from school, it was welcomed. No dance tonight so I could go straight home. I had already planned out my outfit—a short sleeve white lace shirt tucked into a houndstooth skirt, black chunky heel fold over booties, and my mom's navy blue cropped blazer with the sleeves rolled up. I gelled my hair back into half-up pigtails, and put on my gold upside down triangle necklace to match my gold name bracelet.

I looked at myself in the full-length mirror on my closet door. Now if only I had realized I needed glasses sooner, those would have been the perfect finishing touch.

Then I wrote a note to my parents:

Dear Mom & Dad,

I have gone to interview Mr. Fletcher for the school newspaper. I joined the newspaper club, by the way! I know you told me to leave him alone, but as a reporter, this is my duty. If I'm not home by the time you return from work, then go to my PINK jewelry box (not the blue or purple ones) and look for further instructions there.

Love you,

– Holly

I knew my mom wouldn't be happy—I could imagine her hazel eyes popping out of her head. The day Mr. Fletcher moved in, she warned me to stay clear of him until further notice. Today's the day I find out what she meant by that statement. I took a circle rose gold magnet and attached my note to the fridge, put my iPhone (to audio record him), notepad with my questions and holographic pen inside my plaid mini backpack and left. I walked exactly 13 steps—*oh, no, 13 is an unlucky number!*

Then I stood outside of Mr. Fletcher's front door sweating buckets with my hand resting on the bronze knocker. After what seemed like an eternity, a squirrel came and perched itself right on top of the wall that lined the walkway. It sprawled on its stomach, sharp eyes staring down at me. The squirrel twitched like it was going to jump on me and scared me so that I lost my balance and fell to the ground with a crash. At that exact moment, Harper and Xailoh stormed up the stairs from the street and over to me. Harper brandishing her brother's little league baseball bat above her head and Xailoh wearing red boxing gloves so big they were in danger of slipping off. However, it was their all-black tight fitting outfits and caps that really made them look ridiculously suspicious.

"What happened? Are you okay?" Xailoh panted.

"We're ready to kick some b-u-t-t!" Harper said, spelling out the last word.

"Are you here to rob me?" I laughed nervously.

"We're here to help you," Harper fired back.

"Sorry, guys, but didn't I tell you not to come?" I asked though slightly relieved.

"Of course we were going to come."

"Harper just recruited me and told me to wear all black," Xailoh said sheepishly.

"His mom kickboxes, I just knew he had to bring

them," added Harper. "Anyway, where is this wizard? We're ready for battle."

"Okay," I held up a hand. "First of all, I need him to believe this is an interview—that's why I'm sporting my best reporter look and I have my list of questions, notepad and recorder," I said holding up my iPhone. "Second of all, while I may be a bossy little trickster of a friend, this guy could be dangerous and I don't want anything to happen to either of you. So as your friend, I'm asking you to leave." I placed my hand on one of each of their shoulders and led them down the steps and onto the street.

I went back to Mr. Fletcher's door, heart beating wickedly fast, goosebumps crawling up my arms. My father's voice "Stay clear of Mr. Fletcher" rang through my head. *What if beyond this door, the mystery was so awful I wouldn't be allowed to leave ... alive?*

Chapter 10

I REACHED FOR the bronze door knocker, which resembled a rabbit, and knocked it three times. Then a buzzing sound made me jump. I looked down, it was my Apple Watch giving me the same warning sound it makes when they force me to run a mile at school. Woah! My heart rate was dangerously high, pushing 180 beats per minute. I started taking deep breaths to calm down.

Why wasn't he coming to the door? Maybe he is one of those people with really bad hearing. Yeah, he is definitely one of those people. Right?

I was so caught up with my thoughts, and staring at the squirrel who was still there, that I didn't notice Mr. Fletcher standing right outside his door staring at me. I jumped at the sight of him.

"Oh, uh, Mr. Fl-letcher, how…" I coughed… "lovely it is to finally meet you!" I said, faking cheerfulness. "I live next door and was just wondering if I-I could uh, inter-view you for my um, school newspaper."

I was bracing for him to yell or turn me into a toad, until I realized he looked nothing as I imagined. Although he was old, he had kind, blue eyes, a nice mustache that curls up at the tips and tortoise rimmed glasses.

"Of course you can interview me. I can't imagine why you would want to, but that would be just, *lovely*," he said all of this with a British accent, "Well, come in, Holly!"

"Oh, thank you," I said, my cheeks turning red. "Wait, how did you know my name was Holly?"

"Your pretty gold bracelet of course! How about you come inside," Mr. Fletcher said, a broad smile crossing his face. I followed him inside where he led me to his dark living room—dark wood floors, a big brown Chesterfield leather sofa and chairs, and a beautifully ornate black iron rod fireplace. The flowery rug and large crystal jar of gumdrops added a hint of color to an otherwise dark brown room.

He directed me to take a seat on the large brown stud-ded sofa. As soon as he sat down across from me, he popped back up, "How very rude of me! Can I offer you some hot cocoa?"

It's not exactly cold outside so the hot cocoa threw me, but it would be impolite to say no, "Ah, sure, thanks."

After he left, I took a closer look around the room. There were flowers in the corner giving off a potent smell. He also had "interesting" papier-mâché figures, such as snowmen, rabbit, squirrels, trees, and bicycles. Upon closer inspection, the area rug also appeared to include these same figures hidden in the floral design. As I kneeled down to get a better look, I noticed something underneath the couch: a doll house that looked identical to the one I saw in my mom's office. But I couldn't be sure. I reached for it, my fingers grabbing a tiny metal piece, enabling me to bring it closer to me. Once I looked at the metal piece between my fingers, it was unmistakably the bronze rabbit knocker from Mr. Fletcher's front door. I realized, *this isn't a doll house, it's a model home.* I looked for the living room and found a miniature version of the room I was now sitting in. So much detail! But how could this possibly have been the same model home I saw in my mom's office?

It can't so it isn't, I told myself as I pushed it back underneath the couch where I found it, realizing how odd it would look if Mr. Fletcher walked in at this exact moment. I got up and I walked over to his mantel with many framed photos, mostly of a cute-as-a-button older lady who must be his wife and of a little blond girl on horseback.

He came back carrying a tray with two hot cocoas. Hearing him approach I gathered up all my courage and asked, "Is this your daughter?"

"I unfortunately don't remember, but my doctor said she is my niece and I used to call her Pebbles."

"Oh" I replied. *How is it possible he doesn't remember his niece? What happened to her? Did he do something to her? What kind of doctor?* I wanted to ask him all of these questions but was afraid I might face the same fate.

I took a deep breath, "Do you have any idea where Pebbles is now?"

"Who? Oh yes, Pepples, my doctor says she's close by."

Hmm, there is a graveyard only a few blocks away ... Fixated on his lovely fireplace, I realized something odd: the black iron rod gate wasn't a screen at all, it was bolted to the wall. What would be the point of that? Unless it's not a fireplace at all ... but rather a dungeon for children. Why did I tell my Xailoh and Harper to leave?

I nervously sat down and looked at the hot cocoa he had placed in front of me, steaming hot. What if he poisoned it? Should I distract him and switch mugs?

"Did you say you wanted to do an interview?" he said.

"Oh, yes, yes," my mind blank, I fumbled to unzip my backpack for my notes and blurted out the first question that came to mind, "How old are you?" I asked trying to act professional and not letting my fear seep into my speech.

Mr. Fletcher looked at his wrist which had a gold bracelet on it and said, "72." *What! That was exceeding standards!*

"Where were you born?" I asked mimicking my mom when she runs into clients from work.

Once again he looked at his bracelet which I could see had lots of indentations on it. "London."

"London! I love London! I went there for summer vacation last year!" I replied.

"Really! What was your favorite thing you saw?" he asked excitedly.

"I *loooved* The Making Of Harry Potter!"

"So you're a Potterhead?"

"The biggest Potterhead," I replied proudly.

"Then do you want to see something?"

"Sure," I said, my original fear now wrestling with my Potter exuberance.

"Wait here, I'll be right back!" he said getting up with the agility of a thirty-five year old. *He must exercise!* I was impressed and starting to relax a bit, but that didn't stop me from taking this opportunity to switch the drinks. Better to be safe than dead.

I could hear Mr. Fletcher's loud footsteps and out of breath, he said, "Come look!"

I walked over and I saw a first edition Harry Potter *series* signed by J.K. Rowling! "It's not … " I was shaking out of excitement and fear.

"Oh but it is," he replied.

"How?" I asked in total shock.

"Would you like to hold them?"

"Yes!" I gushed trying to calm myself even though my head was going crazy and my watch started beeping again! I took the first book out of his hands and held it, but my hands were trembling so much that I dropped it with a loud *THUNK!*

"NOOOOO!" I yelled out.

Within seconds, the door flew open and in walked Harper and Xailoh looking like burglars.

Chapter 11

"THAT'S IT!" HARPER said using her outside voice.

"I don't know what your game is but, but ... " Xailoh stuttered.

"You're not fooling anyone!" Harper jumped in.

I wasn't sure what to feel—relief? embarrassment?—but tried to pretend everything was normal, "Mr. Fletcher, these are my best friends Harper and Xailoh. This is Mr. Fletcher and he was just showing me his really cool first edition ... Wait didn't you guys leave?"

"Oh for heaven's sake, did you really think we were going to leave you alone with him after everything you said about him?" Harper asked loudly while rolling her eyes.

I saw the saddest look on Mr. Fletcher's face and realized I had misread this entire situation. He wasn't going to poison me or throw me in his dungeon. The anxiety faded away and all I felt was embarrassment.

Mr. Fletcher set the books down and stood up. Xailoh's gloved hands were up and the Harper's hands still clutched the bat.

"Don't you even think about it," Harper said. I wanted to crawl under the rug.

"I'm sorry I seem to have provoked you, but my name is Mr. Fletcher. Would you like some hot cocoa?"

Xailoh and Harper looked confused by Mr. Fletcher's behavior.

"They would love some," I replied on their behalf.

"Two hot cocoas coming right up," Mr. Fletcher said then walked out.

"So was that … "

"Mr. Fletcher?" Harper finished, "you know Mr, 'stay away from him he's evil' dude?'" Harper clarified.

"Yep, crazy right? And he has a first edition Harry Potter series! I accidentally dropped it and that's why I yelled 'No.'"

"Wait, for realz?" Xailoh asked, his eyes getting very big along with Harper's.

"Yes!" I replied beaming.

"OMG!" Harper said, falling back against the wall pretending to faint. As she fell against the wall, she must have pushed a button that opened up an enormous two-story room behind the fireplace.

"What's that?" I asked pointing to the giant opening. Then I realized, this must be the room that borders my bedroom. I could even see the paper thin wall from the other side of my bedroom.

"I was wondering the same thing," Xailoh said.

Harper got up and walked into the room, Xailoh and I tailing behind.

"Wow! Are these virtual reality headsets?" Harper asked.

"No way, there are like ten of them!" Xailoh replied.

We walked into the huge opening through the wall. It was really dark but we could still make out a canopy bed against one of the walls and cushions, lamps and poufs scattered about. There were about ten headsets and also a huge flat screen TV on one of the walls hooked to a computer.

I was approaching one of the headsets when I heard Mr. Fletcher, "I see you have found my VR room."

"Busted," Xailoh whispered under his breath.

"Well come on, let me show you how it works!" Mr. Fletcher said leading us over to the head sets. Not at all the reaction we expected. He fiddled with the computer for a bit then strapped the headsets onto each of our heads, told us which buttons to press and suddenly we were in another world, it was like Ready Player One but hopefully without the "our world is destroyed" thing.

In my virtual reality, I walked towards a cushion to sit

down and sat on a real cushion (I think). The floors were marble and the room was modern. A daybed sat in the corner of the room, a canopy hanging over. A lump in the middle of the daybed grew larger and larger until it was revealed to be a giant bunny. He came over to me and gave me a (wet?) kiss on the cheek. There we were in the middle of a forest filled with sparkling waterfalls, dancing animals, and a psychedelic rainbow of neon lights swirling all around us. The sensory overload became too much and we needed to take our headsets off.

Xailoh, being a VR genius, had some questions, "Since there are other games on the Oculus, how does this room adjust to the different scenes?"

"Oh, what a marvelous question! I suggest you all step away from the center of the room and outside of the blue tape." Mr. Fletcher replied, his English accent really shining through.

When I looked down I realized that there was blue tape and hurriedly stepped behind it. What happened next was truly mind blowing—the center of the room just flipped, literally flipped, upside down, revealing a new setup. "This room has hundreds of 'floor plans' that it can change into, as well as several other customizable settings!"

We were astonished, and yet I could feel the clock ticking on my article and knew I needed to get back to the interview.

"Wow! This is all so cool! However I really think we should get back to the interview," I said. I hurried out of the room and they followed me. Mr. Fletcher closed the opening in the wall.

"Your hot cocoa is right there for you," he said motioning toward the cups of cocoa sitting on the glass table in the pink, turquoise, and purple cups. We picked up the cocoa and started taking sips, enjoying all the rich, chocolatey AMAZINGNESS! I went back to asking questions once we had all settled in. Harper, Xailoh and I on one couch, Mr. Fletcher on the other.

"Are you married?"

Mr. Fletcher looked at his bracelet then frowned. "I am afraid I don't know." Out of the corner of my eye, I could see Xailoh and Harper exchanging a curious look.

I had to ask, "Why do you keep looking at your bracelet every time I ask a question?"

"The doctors gave me this bracelet and it contains many basic facts of my life."

At that moment, there was a knock at the door. I was shocked because I had never seen him with another living person.

"I'll get it," said Mr. Fletcher looking just as shocked as I did.

"Okie-dokie" I replied.

Chapter 12

Mr. Fletcher opened the door and said, "I'm sorry, do I know you?"

As soon as we heard the woman at the door reply, we all looked at each other nervously.

"I'm Lilliana, your niece," my mom said solemnly.

"What? My *mom* is Pebbles?" I blurted out to my friends, jumped up and ran to the door.

"I'm sorry, I don't understand," he said slowly and confused.

"Uncle Fletcher, I'm Pebbles, I know you don't remember me because you have amnesia, but please believe me."

Wait wait wait … WHAT? Okay I needed some answers.

"Mom, I thought you said your uncle was you know … dead," I whispered the last word.

"Sorry, that was just a convenient lie I came up with. I was mad at my uncle for the longest time because he killed my cactus when I was in college, and since my major was botany it was kind of a big deal." My mom took a deep breath before continuing, "But when I heard a bird feeder fell on his head and gave him amnesia, I knew it was time to bury the hatchet. Since he was living in the English countryside all alone, the doctors thought he should move to be near family but at the same time, they warned me to give him plenty of space because the ill will between us could hurt his recovery and cause more harm than good."

At that moment Mr. Fletcher's face transformed and he rushed toward my mom and said, "Oh, how I've missed you!"

"You remember me!" Mom said, suddenly the glow of her younger self returning to her face. "The doctor did say that all of your memories could rush back if something triggers them."

Then Mom looked at me, "I'm sorry I lied to you, it just never seemed like the right time to come clean about everything."

"Like what you were doing at the hospital the other night?

"Well … " my mom started. "I came home to find all those terrible smelling wolfsbane candles and I panicked that Uncle Fletcher's condition was getting worse, so I took him to see his psychiatrist. Dad met me there. We still don't know why he did it."

"I do." A lightbulb seemed to go off in Mr.—I mean Uncle Fletcher's head. "Even before the amnesia, I've always had some difficulty distinguishing reality from my dreams, exacerbated by how much time I spend developing virtual worlds. I've never really gotten over my wife Aubrey who left me, and in my dream thought I needed to light hundreds of her favorite frankincense candles to win her back." There was a long pause.

"But those were wolfsbane candles, not frankincense," Mom said.

A big smile stretched across Xailoh's face, "I told you that scent was definitely wolfsbane!"

I gave him a high five.

"I have one last question: I noticed a very detailed model home in my mom's office and the same exact one underneath Great Uncle Fletcher's—can I just call you Uncle Fletcher?—sofa. "

"Yes, you may." *Ha, he's already correcting my grammar!*

"They're duplicates," my mom explained. "Both are exact replicas of this townhome when Uncle Fletcher and Aunt Aubrey used to live here decades ago. Next door to my mother, your grandmother who passed before you were born. She lived in the home we live in now. His doctors in England sent it to me so I could try and set everything up the way he and Aunt Aubrey did. They thought it would help with his recovery process to be surrounded by familiar things at a time when he was most happy."

"But sometimes when I entered my home and saw everything the way it used to be, I thought Aubrey was still in my life."

So that's who he's been talking to! "Gosh, I wish we could hang out all night and celebrate, but I need to get home and write up this article while it's still fresh in my head."

"Of course! This was the most incredible night of my new life, one I will never forget," chuckled Uncle Fletcher.

Chapter 13

MY ODDBALL NEIGHBOR
By Holly Woodsnoff

MY NAME IS Holly Woodsnoff. In four days, I will turn 13, and for my entire life I thought my mom and dad were my only living family. I just learned that the strange and annoying neighbor who moved in next door about a month ago is actually my Great Uncle Fletcher. While it's true that he has always been "a little off" according to my mom, he is not at all scary and actually quite amazing.

Here, let me give you some background on my Great Uncle: he graduated from Yale and was valedictorian of his class. In his 20s, he fell in love with his tailor, my Great Aunt Aubrey. They married and started a clothing business together and got rich when they sold it a few years later for millions and millions of dollars. Never having to work again, they spent their time reading, gardening and riding horses. Eventually my Great Aunt Aubrey fell out of favor with that lifestyle (I have no idea why) and wanted to explore the world on her own. No one has heard from her since.

So two months ago, when a heavy bird feeder fell on my Great Uncle Fletcher's head in the middle of the English countryside where he lived all alone, there was no one around to help him. His doctors arranged for him to move back to his townhouse in Santa Monica next door to his only living relative, his niece "Pebbles" a.k.a my mom.

His amnesia caused him to start talking to people who are no longer around, such as my Great Aunt Aubrey. He's also a "virtual reality geek"—as my mom puts it—and even has a special room which—*lucky me*—I share a wall with. That's where all the annoying sounds and lights emanate from every evening just as I'm trying to fall asleep.

This story is a perfect example of don't judge a book by its cover. If I hadn't joined the newspaper club for an excuse to interview my mysterious neighbor, I would have thought he was a big scary monster forever and not my incredibly Great Uncle Fletcher.

Now that he understands how much noise his virtual reality games make, he installed a brand new sound-proof wall and we have a rule that he can't play late at night.

So the other lessons here are, One: If you don't know 'em don't judge 'em. Two: Get the full story, which leads into Three: Parents, your kids can handle more than you think they can, and are also a lot smarter than you think. Just make your lives easy and tell your kids the **full** story!

Chapter 14

THE AUDITORIUM WAS bustling with life. Kids were standing by their science fair projects ready to present to any parent, student, or judge willing to listen.

Xailoh and I were waiting for our turn to present our project to the room. I had a feeling I'd have to present it myself given Xailoh's serious stage fright issues.

I was wearing a silver romper, complemented by a light pink jacket, and tan wedge sandals. Meanwhile Xailoh was looking very European, wearing long shorts with yellow and blue vertical stripes, a yellow Lacoste shirt. I obviously picked out this outfit for him.

Ms. Paley announced, "For our seventh contestant I would like to announce Xailoh and Holly!"

I looked at Xailoh who gave a slight head shake, so I proceeded to the stage alone. From the stage, I saw Mom, Dad, Great Uncle Fletcher, as well as the rows of science projects. I also saw, Harper, Xailoh, Annabella, and Charlie.

I took out my phone and started scrolling, as I waited for Ms. Paley to scold me.

Right on cue, Ms. Paley cleared her throat and said, "You can start whenever you would like, Holly. We're all waiting."

"Oh, hello there!" I said acting surprised. "I'm sure this is a common sight for most … who am I kidding? For *all* of you." I pursed my lips and the audience laughed. "Actually after doing this science project on social media habits with my amazing partner Xailoh, I learned that, not surprisingly, my age group of 12 to 15 year olds spends the most time on social media. Who would have thought?" I rolled my eyes again eliciting more laughs from the audience.

I continued explaining how we learned that the youngest group (under 12 years old) and oldest group (over 55 years old) use social media the least and have the most positive feelings about the social media platform. So maybe less time spent is better!

After finishing my presentation and getting lots of laughs and applause I took an exaggerated bow and walked down the stairs of the stage back to Xailoh, knowing we had nailed it and had a real shot at winning The Science Cup.

And I was right. Much to their disappointment, Annabella and Charlie got second. Annabella walked right up to Xailoh and started gushing about what an incredible job *he* did and how nice he looked. Xailoh's parents who rarely show any kind of emotion, were overjoyed, gave him a big hug and told him how proud they were.

I couldn't believe my good luck. My mom and dad had their arms around me and my Great Uncle Fletcher was waiting to give me a hug, too. I looked up at him, "Can we celebrate with one of your hot chocolates?"

About the Author

ADELE BEATRIZ CIOCIOLA was born in 2006 and lives with her mom and dad in Santa Monica. She has the best friends ever and loves Harry Potter, school, dancing, reading, writing, and DIYing! You can follow her on Instagram or YouTube @AdeleDIYs, or visit her website AdeleDIYs.com.